EVA ERIKSSON

MOLLY GOES SHOPPING

Translated by Elisabeth Kallick Dyssegaard

R&S BOOKS

Stockholm   New York   London   Adelaide   Toronto

Molly has gotten so smart lately.
Now she's going to the store to shop.
Can she really go that far all by herself?
"Buy a bag of beans," says Grandma.
"That's easy to carry."

Molly holds Grandma's coin purse in her hand.
Everyone will be able to tell she's going shopping.
Not everyone is smart enough to go shopping.

There are a lot of ladies in the store.
Once in a while a new lady comes in,
and some of the old ladies leave. No one sees Molly.
How does this work, anyway?
When will it be Molly's turn?

When a really long time has passed
and many ladies have come and gone,
it's Molly's turn.

What is she getting?
"A bag . . ." A bag of something. What was it?
"A bag . . ."
Now everyone is looking at Molly. What good does that do?
Can't they look at something else?
"A bag . . ."

"Perhaps a bag of potatoes?
Are you getting a bag of potatoes?" asks the clerk.
"Yes," says Molly.

There. She has shopped.
That went well.
Now she just has to go back the same way.
The bag is rather big to carry.
It is also rather heavy.

A big, heavy bag—now everyone can really see
that she has been shopping.

What an incredibly heavy bag!
And so big!

Why did she have to buy
such a heavy bag?
Silly Grandma.

Grandma is surprised when she sees the bag.
"Sweetheart, what is this?"

"Potatoes? No wonder it was heavy.
But, sweetie, you were supposed to buy beans.
A bag of beans."

"Beans! That's what I said.
I said I wanted beans, but she gave me potatoes anyway."
"She gave you potatoes even though you asked for beans?
What kind of person is she!"

"Yes, she was so dumb, that person.
'I don't want potatoes,' I said. 'I want beans.'
'No, you are getting potatoes,' she said."
"She has some nerve! To give you such
a bag to carry. What was she thinking?"

"I'm going to go and give her
a piece of my mind!"

Now Grandma goes back to the store with the
bag of potatoes. She is very angry at the clerk.

Grandma soon returns.
She is no longer angry at the clerk.
"You said you wanted potatoes.
Why did you lie to me?"
Molly can't answer that.

"Did you forget what you were supposed to buy?"
"Sort of."
"That can happen to anyone.
But you must not lie anymore," says Grandma.
No, Molly will never do that again.

Grandma asks Molly if she would like to go and get them
each a Danish pastry for tea.
Yes, she can do that. Now she is on top of things and strong again,
and pastries are easy to carry.

The bakery is not far.
Pastry, pastry, pastry,
you can't forget pastry!

When Molly gets there, she hasn't forgotten
the pastry. But now there's something else.
The coin purse. It's gone!

Molly runs back to Grandma as fast
as possible. How could this happen?
She cries very quietly.

Then she cries loudly and a lot.
Grandma thinks she's probably just dropped
the coin purse on the sidewalk.
Didn't she see it on the way back?
"No," screams Molly. "It's been stolen!"

Grandma goes out
with her to look for it.
When they have gotten halfway
to the bakery, Molly finds it.
How lucky!

Grandma goes home and Molly walks
the rest of the way by herself.

Molly doesn't have to wait long.
Soon it's her turn.
The coin purse is still in her hand.
Now she just has to ask for: "Two . . . two . . ."

"Cream puffs, perhaps?
Perhaps you and Grandma are having
a cream puff party today?
They've just come out of the oven."
Molly thinks she recognizes them.

The clerk puts them in a box.
Can Molly carry it?
Yes, she can.
She's carried worse.

But a box?
Usually there's not a box
when Grandma shops.
Usually there's a bag.
Is something
wrong again?

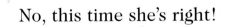

No, this time she's right!